ABOUT THIS BOOK
ADVENTURE IN GRANADA
Walter Dean Myers

Chris and Ken are enjoying their stay in Spain while their
mother, famous anthropologist Carla Arrow, works on her
study of Gypsy family life—until the brothers' friend Pedro
is accused of stealing a valuable Spanish cross. Suddenly the
boys find themselves caught up in a race to recover the cross
and to clear their friend's name. But the real thieves aren't
too happy with Chris and Ken's interference, and they'll do
anything to make sure that the Spanish treasure doesn't get
in the hands of the Arrows!

There's never a dull moment when the Arrows are on
the trail! Traveling from beautiful churches to dangerous
mountain roads, Chris and Ken find adventure at every
turn in this fast-paced story of action and intrigue.

ALSO BY WALTER DEAN MYERS

The Black Pearl and the Ghost
Fast Sam, Cool Clyde, and Stuff
The Golden Serpent
The Hidden Shrine
The Legend of Tarik
Mojo and the Russians
Motown and Didi
The Nicholas Factor
Won't Know Till I Get There
The Young Landlords

ADVENTURE IN GRANADA

BY

WALTER DEAN MYERS

PUFFIN BOOKS

PUFFIN BOOKS
Viking Penguin Inc., 40 West 23rd Street, New York, New York 10010, U.S.A.
Penguin Books Ltd, Harmondsworth, Middlesex, England
Penguin Books Australia Ltd, Ringwood, Victoria, Australia
Penguin Books Canada Limited, 2801 John Street, Markham, Ontario, Canada L3R 1B4
Penguin Books (N.Z.) Ltd, 182–190 Wairau Road, Auckland 10, New Zealand

First published in Puffin Books 1985
Published simultaneously in Canada

Copyright © Walter Dean Myers, 1985
All rights reserved
Printed in the United States of America by R. R. Donnelley & Sons Co.,
Harrisonburg, Virginia

Set in Trump

Library of Congress catalog card number: 85-43041
(CIP data available)
ISBN 0 14 03.2011 3

ADVENTURE IN GRANADA

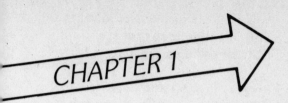

CHAPTER 1

"But what would I want with the cross?" Pedro Barcia shrugged. His dark eyes widened as he spoke. "I was happy to have it at the church. I didn't take it."

"When something's taken from a church it's pretty serious," Ken said. Ken and Pedro were the same age, fourteen, but Ken was taller. "I guess the police have to ask questions."

"I think it's because I'm a Gypsy," Pedro said. "In Spain we Gypsies have a hard time. Those police kept me all day. It is almost ten o'clock now."

"Anyway, they finally let you go," I said. I was hoping the dark road we were on led back to the hotel.

"Do you think they would have so much nerve to hold me?" Pedro said. "I am very fierce when I am angry!"

"I bet you are," I said.

3

"Watch it!" Ken said as the headlights of a car swept over us.

The three of us stepped off the road to wait until the car passed. I could tell it was coming at great speed.

"Hey, it's headed right for us!" Ken shouted.

"Jump!"

We dove out of the way as the car narrowly missed us.

"You blind or something?!" Ken yelled. The car screeched to a halt on the dark Spanish street.

"He stopped!" Pedro said. "Now I tell him something!"

"Wait a minute!" I was still on my knees by the side of the road when I saw the car backing up. "Let's get out of here!"

The car came speeding toward us again. I jumped up and headed toward a clump of trees on my right. Ken and Pedro were right behind me. The car screeched to a stop, then turned off the road after us. Somebody was trying to run us down!

"Run!" I shouted.

The lights of the car were on us and the roar of the engine grew louder. Looking back, I saw Ken fall, struggle to his feet, and barely make it out of the path of the oncoming car.

At last I reached the trees. Pedro was beside me. Ken joined us as the car turned around and headed back for the road. In moments it was gone.

"Hey, what was that all about?" Ken's chest was heaving.

"I think," I said, "that somebody just tried to kill us!"

We all spent a few minutes catching our breath. Ken

kept looking at me the way he does sometimes, and pushing his glasses up on his nose.

"Chris, were you scared?" he asked.

"I think," I said, still breathing heavily, "that I'm the scaredest seventeen-year-old in Spain."

"Pedro, you want to stay with us tonight?" Ken asked. "I don't think Mom will mind."

"Good idea," I said.

"I will stay with you if you are nervous," Pedro said.

Ken and I had met Pedro on our first day in Spain. Mom had done some sightseeing with us, mostly around the palace of the Moors, the fabulous Alhambra. Pedro was selling postcards and soft drinks there. Later I went back by myself to take pictures. Pedro had told me the best time to come.

"Early in the morning," he said. "Before the tourist buses come. Once they get there the place is too full of people to take pictures."

My mom is an anthropologist and studies different kinds of family life. Two days after we arrived in Spain Mom was making arrangements to go study the Gypsy families in the hills outside of Granada. Pedro was a Gypsy and seemed to be a pretty neat guy. That's why it surprised us when he was questioned about the disappearance of the Cruzada Cross.

The cross is famous. It's been in the village church for hundreds of years. When a new priest comes to the parish, there's a ceremony welcoming him to the parish, the church, and the cross. It's called the Cruzada Cross because it's believed to have been among the things that the Crusaders carried with them hundreds of years ago.

"I walked into the church that night to pay a little visit," Pedro told us. "I go in and I see a woman standing near the altar. I see her holding the cross up and I say *buenos noces*, but then I think to myself, Pedro, suppose this lady is a saint coming to this church and that's why she's holding the cross. After all, it's a pretty heavy cross. So I close my eyes and say one 'Hail Mary,' and when I open them again she's gone."

"Then what happened?" Ken asked.

"Then I go to where she was standing and I see the cross is gone, so I figure it has to be a miracle. Then I go to my uncle's house."

"That's it?" Ken asked.

"Almost," Pedro said. "I went back to the church to see if anybody else knows about the miracle, and the police catch me."

I had a feeling we weren't getting the whole story, but I didn't say anything.

Mom had booked us into the Washington Irving Hotel, which was right across from the Alhambra. It was an old hotel but kind of nice. By the time we got there we had decided not to tell Mom about the car. We didn't want her to worry.

"I thought I was going to have trouble with you guys in Spain," Mom said. "Where have you been?"

"At Pedro's house," Ken piped up. "He's got a real neat place."

"I think the time just got away from us a bit," I said. "Anyway, we told you about Pedro being accused of stealing the cross, didn't we?"

"You didn't say he was accused," Mom said. "You just said that some people *thought* he did it."

"I swear upon my mother's grave that I did not take it," Pedro said. He had his hand across his heart.

"Oh, is your mother dead?" Mom asked.

"No, she went to Toledo to find a job," Pedro said.

"Since Pedro doesn't have much to do, I thought he could spend a few days with us," I said.

"I don't see why not," Mom answered.

"Anyway," Ken said, "he's been feeling a little rundown recently. Maybe he can rest better here."

"He looks fine to me," Mom said, putting her hand on Pedro's forehead.

"I think what Ken needs," I said, "is to get a few new pistachios—the ones he's been using to think with are getting a little used."

"Thank goodness!" Mom said. "I'd hate to leave you guys in the morning if you weren't fighting. You'd have nothing to do!"

Mom left just after daybreak. I heard her come into the room and saw her kiss Ken while he was still asleep. She touched Pedro lightly on the head, smiled, and came over to where I was lying in the brass single bed.

"You have Profesora Velásquez's number if you want to reach me," Mom said. "If there are any problems—"

"—even the smallest ones that I don't feel are important," I said, finishing the sentence I knew she was going to say.

"Even the smallest ones that you don't feel are important," she said, ignoring me, "you call me. And please don't let your brother start any major insurrections."

"I'll try not to, Mom," I said.

She kissed me quickly, held my hand for a long moment, and then left. She had told us the night before that she would be living with Profesora Velásquez among the Gypsy families for at least a week. I watched her cab pull away from the sidewalk below just as the birds turned up the volume of their chattering to full blast.

I couldn't get back to sleep so I decided to get dressed. The sky was overcast, and I was thinking about taking my camera over to the palace when somebody started banging on the door.

"*La Policia!*" came a heavy voice.

The banging woke Ken and Pedro, and we all looked at one another. Then Ken pointed toward the closet, and Pedro went into it.

"*La Policia!*" The banging continued.

I took a deep breath and opened the door. Two police officers, one with a fancy uniform, stood in the doorway.

"Señor Abreu, the desk clerk, says that you have an additional guest in your room. Someone who sleeps here without paying." The policeman in the fancy uniform put his face close to mine. He had bad breath. "Is that true?"

"Just my mother, my brother, and I stay here," I said. "My mother's Dr. Carla Arrow, an anthropologist."

"Tell your mother that Captain Ismael Rodriguez-Vega wants to see her," the captain said.

"She's not here right now," I said.

"So who is here right now?" the captain asked. Behind

him I could see the desk clerk. He was the one who had told the captain that Pedro was in our room.

"My brother and me," I said.

Captain Rodriguez pushed past me into the room and started looking around.

"You can't just come in here like this," I said, trying to sound convincing.

Captain Rodriguez snapped his fingers twice and pointed under one of the beds. His assistant looked under both beds, then went into the next room and did the same thing. I had my heart in my mouth. He gave me a look and then pointed toward the closet. It wasn't the one Pedro was in, but I swallowed hard anyway. His assistant looked into it and took out Ken's stuffed frog.

He showed it to the captain, and the captain slapped him with his gloves.

"Stupid!" he said.

We went back into the other room, and the captain pointed to the closet Pedro had jumped into. Ken jumped in front of it.

"My *mother's* things are in there," Ken said.

It didn't work. The assistant gave Ken a push and opened the closet. It was empty!

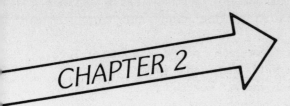

CHAPTER 2

I stood in the doorway and gave the captain, his assistant, and the oily desk clerk the meanest look I could muster as I watched them enter the elevator. Then I rushed back into the room.

"Are you looking for me, *amigo?*"

I looked down and saw Pedro looking up at me from under the bed.

"When I saw the police look under this bed and then walk into the other room," Pedro said, wriggling out from his hiding spot, "I left the closet and hid here."

We decided that it wouldn't be safe for Pedro to stay with us any longer. The desk clerk would be looking for him, and he wouldn't always be so lucky in hiding from the police. Ken and I took the elevator to the lobby. Pedro came down by way of the stairs. When we saw that Captain Rodriguez had left, we signaled to Pedro, and he came walking slowly down the stairs. Señor Abreu, the desk clerk, turned red and fixed his mouth so that he looked like he was trying to keep a frog from jumping out of it.

Pedro's Uncle Enero got back from Malaga later in the day. Pedro took us to his small repair shop.

"This is the whole thing?" Ken asked.

It wasn't much more than a small room. Pedro's uncle was working on a pickup truck he owned that was parked on the street. We went in and Pedro took some warm sodas from under a bench and passed them around. They were nearly hot, and I hate hot sodas, but I didn't want to make Pedro feel bad by refusing one.

"Malaga is nice this time of year," Uncle Enero said. He was a short, round man with enormous arms and a mustache that was bigger on one side than the other. "If I were a rich man I would live there. They have lots of motorbikes in Malaga."

"Why do you want to live in Malaga?" Pedro asked. "Granada is better."

"Who in Granada knows how wonderful my hands are?" he said, holding his hands before him. His fingers were short and stocky and powerful looking. "These hands can play a guitar, can grow the most beautiful roses in the world, can fix anything, can make the best paella in the world!"

"I think your paella is terrible, Uncle," Pedro said.

"Terrible, wonderful, what's the difference?" Uncle Enero said. "Food is food."

"I told Chris and Ken about the cross," Pedro said.

"Do you know why they accuse you of such things?"

Uncle Enero asked. "Because you don't live like a nice person. I come to see you today and the door is open and everything is thrown all over the place. What did you do, lose something?"

"I don't know what you are talking about," Pedro said.

"It sounds as if your place was searched," Ken said.

"Why don't you go and buy some ice for your uncle?" Uncle Enero said. "Be kind to an old man."

"I can't," Pedro said, standing up. "Chris wants to go to the newspaper office and see the stories about the cross being stolen."

"Your uncle must have really great hands," Ken said. "Is he really good on the guitar?"

"Uncle Enero?" Pedro smiled. "He's terrible. He plays guitar like he's strangling it."

"How about growing roses?" I asked.

"He could not grow a weed in a jungle," Pedro said. "And he can't fix motorbikes either."

"Then what does he do?" Ken asked.

"He loves me," Pedro said. "He takes care of my goat."

We went to the office of a newspaper that was published in English and got permission to look at their files. I looked up the day that had the story about the theft of the cross.

FAMOUS CROSS STOLEN

The Cruzada Cross, believed by many to date from the Crusades, was stolen last night from the Church of the Holy Name in the Moneta Diez section of the city. Police Captain Rodriguez vowed that he would have the cross returned by the end of the month. "It has been stolen as a prank," he said.

"There's not a lot about it," I said.

"It's important to us," Pedro said, "because it has been in the church a long time. It's important to Captain Rodriguez, too, because it's the first time he has had his name in the papers for almost two years."

We looked in the newspaper files for more about the theft of the cross, but we didn't find anything else. It didn't make any sense to me that someone would want to steal the cross. Maybe, I thought, Captain Rodriguez was right. Maybe somebody had stolen it as a prank. I just didn't think it was funny.

We had lunch in town and then went with Pedro back to his house. The place was a mess, just as Uncle Enero had said. We helped him clean it up.

"You going to be okay here?" Ken asked.

"Sure," Pedro said. "Most of the time I leave my door open. But now I'll leave it closed. I'll be fine."

I wasn't that sure, and neither was Ken.

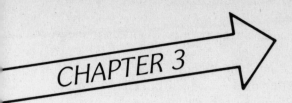

CHAPTER 3

"The obvious question"—Ken wiped the corners of his mouth with his fingers—"is what were they looking for at Pedro's?" We were having sodas in the hotel lobby restaurant. I was having my first and Ken was working on his second.

"It could have been just a robbery," I said. "Don't start with your fantasies."

"Pedro is not a wealthy person," Ken said. "Not only that, but only the large drawers in his house were opened. That means somebody was looking for something large. There were several small drawers that were not dumped out. A thief would look for money."

"Could be," I said.

"Something large like the Cruzada Cross," Ken went on.

"Could be."

"I think we should return to the scene of the crime," Ken said. "Let's go to the church. Maybe we can pick up some kind of clue."

"If the police couldn't pick up a clue, and they know the place, we won't either," I said.

"Perhaps," Ken said. "On the other hand—"

Just then a tall, thin man came up to our table. I looked up at him, and he just smiled. He looked to be over six feet tall, and he was well-dressed. In fact his clothes were kind of formal for the middle of the day. He wore glasses, the sort without rims, so you could see most of his face. I figured him to be about forty. His face was fairly ordinary, except for the scar that ran from just below his ear to the corner of his mouth.

"May I join you?" he asked, pulling out a chair and sitting down.

"Sure, why not?" Ken said, looking at me.

"My name is Erich Bauer. I am a historian. I'm in Spain doing research on Roderick, the last of the great Visigoth kings."

"That's nice," Ken said.

"Are you young men also scholars?"

"In a way," I said. "Why do you ask?"

"Ah!" He leaned back slightly as he smiled, as if I had said something that amused him. "I see you have the scholar's mind. That is good. Well, I have evidence that Roderick's crown, which has been missing for centuries, might be somewhere in this area."

"What kind of evidence?" Ken asked.

"Mmm." Bauer lifted his eyebrows and nodded. "That, too, is an excellent question, but I must beg to deny you the answer. You see, if I were to surrender the evidence and you came across the crown before I did, you would publish your accounts at my expense."

"And is that why you came over?" I asked. "To see if we were looking for this crown of . . . who did you say?"

"King Roderick," Bauer said. "His defeat in battle by the Moorish general Tarik marked the end of the Visigoth reign. It's all quite fascinating, really. But no, I didn't think you were looking for the crown. I imagine you have your own project, but I just thought I would tell you of my own search in case we could be of mutual benefit. What is your area of study?"

"My mother's an anthropologist," Ken said. "She's really important."

"Yes, yes." Bauer rubbed his chin with his fingertips. "I'm sure she must be. But I haven't seen her with you."

"She's away for the week," Ken said. "Studying Gypsy family life. But she'll be back next Wednesday."

"I see," Bauer said. "Well, if you hear anything about a crown, you'll let me know. I'm in the hotel."

Bauer reached into his inside coat pocket and produced a card. Then he got up quickly, bowed, and walked away.

"I guess I do look a little like a scholar," Ken said.

"That guy gives me the creeps," I said. "Did you see that scar across his face?"

"I saw it," Ken said.

"And why would some guy we've never seen before walk up to us, a seventeen-year-old and an undersized fourteen-year-old, and ask us if we're scholars?"

"It's probably just that some people can recognize intelligence faster than others," Ken said. "And I'm *not* undersized."

"Why has he been watching us?"

"Illogical, my good man," Ken said, hopping back into his Sherlock Holmes role. "If you have never seen him before, you cannot know that he has been watching us."

"He's been watching us long enough to know that Mom isn't around," I said. "I don't like it. You think that computer nut friend of yours is still in London?"

"Ian Knowles?" Ken was noisily sucking the last bits of lemonade from the corner of his glass. "He said his father is letting him work at the British Museum all summer, so I guess he's still there. Why?"

"Let's write to him and ask him if the museum knows anything about this Cruzada Cross."

We decided to send a telegram to Ken's friend. Ian is a quirky kid, a little like Ken. He spends half his time sitting in front of a computer terminal and the other half reading computer magazines.

The cable was simple and to the point:

ANY VALUE IN CRUZADA CROSS OF GRANADA STOP
IS CROWN OF RODERICK POSSIBLY IN GRANADA?

We took a jitney to the telegraph office. The lines were down, but the clerk told us that the cable would be sent within the hour.

"Why you send this cable?" The cable clerk was a fairly old guy with a heavy accent. "You have the cross?"

"No," Ken said. "We were just wondering if it had any value."

"Why do you care if you don't have it?"

"Do you have it?" Ken asked.

"Me?" The old man straightened up and pulled at his vest. "The cable will be sent as soon as the lines are open."

The clerk turned away with a series of harumphs, and I could see that Ken had ticked him off.

Granada is a bustling town with many businesses and lots of traffic. It's also very hot. The sun felt warm on my skin as we came out onto the street. I stood for a moment, waiting until my eyes got accustomed to the bright sun, and I tried to decide whether this would be a day to go sightseeing. Suddenly Ken grabbed my arm.

"Chris!" He let out a yelp that sounded almost like a dog's bark. "Look who's across the street."

I looked across the street, and there, standing on the corner, was the tall, thin form of Erich Bauer.

"You think he followed us?" I asked Ken.

Ken shrugged.

We walked quickly down the street, staying close to the buildings. When we got to the corner, we turned and saw Bauer go into a store that sold paper goods.

"You know," Ken said, "Now that I think about it, that guy gives me the creeps, too."

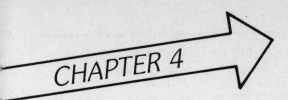

CHAPTER 4

Pedro had mentioned that he would be working in his uncle's shop, so we went there looking for him the next day. We found him putting a tire in a vat of water.

"You trying to drown it?" Ken asked.

"You got to look for the bubbles if you're going to find a leak," Pedro said.

Pedro looked sad, and neither Ken nor I spoke for a while. We watched Pedro turn the tire slowly, looking for bubbles that would show that air was escaping.

"I was thinking that we should go back to the church," Ken said. "Maybe look around to see if we could find a clue or two."

"I don't think so," Pedro said.

Uncle Enero came over and looked at the tire.

"Don't worry so," he said to Pedro. "You've got such

a long face you'll scare your friends away. Everything will be all right."

"What happened?" I asked.

"We got a letter," Uncle Enero said. "They want to take Pedro to Madrid and put him in a home for bad boys. I think that Captain Rodriguez made up that letter to scare Pedro."

"How can they do that?" Ken asked. "They don't have any proof that he took the cross!"

"They have proof I don't go to school too much," Pedro said.

"I'll tell them it is my fault," Uncle Enero said. "I'll tell them that when his mother comes home he will go to school."

"Let's go over to the church, Pedro," Ken said. "Maybe it'll take your mind off the letter."

"Go with your friends," Uncle Enero said. He put a big arm around Pedro's shoulders.

Uncle Enero had a motorbike with a side car. It could have been fifty years old. Maybe even older. The bike itself was red, and the side car was painted gray. I think it was supposed to be silver but never quite made it. It had a western saddle instead of a regular seat, and two rows of leather fringe on both sides. Pedro was allowed to use it, so he, Ken, and I took it to the church. I did the driving, and Ken and Pedro rode in the side car. The leather fringe flapped in the wind, and the muffler produced a noise that sounded like the whine of a jet. It was a pretty wild ride.

The church was a high building with a fairly steep roof and a stucco front. It had huge doors ornamented with brass. The front doors were closed, so we went in through the side entrance.

Two rows of candles burned brightly in front of the altar. On one side of the altar there was a basket in which people had placed coins. On the other side was a larger basket, in which there were eggs, bread, a few onions, and other things that people who couldn't give money would bring.

"Where were you when you saw the cross being taken?" Ken asked in a low voice. When he spoke like that, he sounded almost like Mom.

"In the back," Pedro said. "There, in front of the doors."

"How could you see in this darkness?"

"If I could see well, I would tell you who took the cross. But I know I saw a woman there."

"Are you sure it was a woman?" I asked.

"I think I am sure," Pedro said.

We looked around a bit more, but we didn't find anything. The structure that the Cruzada Cross had sat on was built right into the wall. There was a spot in back of it that looked a little lighter than the rest of the wall, but that was about all.

Pedro still seemed depressed. I could understand why. I sure wouldn't want to be accused of stealing anything. I especially wouldn't want to be accused of stealing something from a church.

Outside, a few women were sitting under a tree, cutting up fruit and putting it into large bowls.

"They're making wine for the holidays," Pedro said.

Several of the women pointed at Pedro and shook their heads.

"Let's go and see if Ian has sent an answer to our cable," Ken said.

"It's only been a day, Ken," I said. "Even Ian needs some time to look up the answers."

"It might have been in the computer," Ken said. "Anyway, what else do we have to do?"

What I wanted to do was to take more pictures of the palace at Granada. It was one of the most beautiful sites in Spain and I hoped that if I took really good pictures, I might be able to get them into a magazine. Mom would be working in Spain for only another few weeks, and I did want to get some pictures in.

We got back onto the motorbike and tried to start it. The engine clicked once, then again, and then died. I kicked the starter twice more, but it sounded as if the battery was dead. That surprised me because it had started so easily before. I got off and checked the battery connections. They were okay.

"Let's push it back to the shop," Pedro said. "My uncle will fix it."

It was a good two miles from the church to the middle of town, but we started off anyway. Most of it was downhill and we all piled on and coasted. The uphill parts were murder. By the time we reached the heart of town we were all dripping with sweat. When Ken suggested again that we stop to see if Ian had answered his cable, I didn't object.

It was getting hotter, and I bought soft drinks from a street vender for Pedro and myself. We sat on the bike, Pedro on the seat with his feet across the handlebars, and me in the side car with my legs dangling over the side. Ken went up to the telegraph office.

It took him ten minutes to get back.

"Any answer?" I asked.

"Something funny happened," Ken said. "There was a fire in the telegraph office yesterday. It still smells pretty bad. The walls were covered with soot."

"When did that happen?" I asked.

"The clerk said it happened about a half hour after we left and so he didn't have a chance to get our cable out," Ken said.

"It's not working today, either?" Pedro asked.

"Oh, it's working all right," Ken said. "But a lot of the messages that were to be sent yesterday were burned in the fire."

"There's an old man in there, right?" Pedro said. "He's got hair on the sides of his head but none on the top, right?"

"Right," Ken said.

"He doesn't smoke or anything," Pedro said. "Why does he have a fire in that place?"

I knew what Ken was thinking. We had seen Erich Bauer outside of the telegraph office right after we had left. Both of us were wondering if he had anything to do with it.

We tried starting the motorbike again, but nothing happened.

Pedro looked at the battery, tapped it with a screwdriver, and tried starting it again. Still nothing. We began pushing the bike toward Uncle Enero's shop. We were just about beat when we got there.

"I hope your uncle can fix it," Ken said.

"I'm just glad I have bus fare back," I said.

The shop was closed and Pedro figured Uncle Enero had gone home or to a restaurant to have dinner. Pedro went around the corner, and a few minutes later the door to the shop opened.

"There is more than one way to get into a place," Pedro said.

Ken gave me a look that I knew meant how come Pedro knows so much about getting into places?

"You think we should try to send the telegram again?" Ken asked.

"I thought you sent it already," I said.

"Ieee!"

We looked up to see Pedro staring at the motorbike. I went over to see what he was staring at. He had taken off the side panel, which covered part of the motor. There, attached to a spark plug with wires, was what looked like a stick of dynamite!

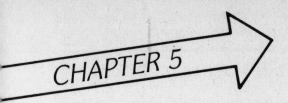

CHAPTER 5

We got out of the shop as quickly as we could. Ken's eyes were very wide, and I knew he was scared. I was scared, too, but I was also mad.

"You sure your Uncle Enero likes you?" Ken asked Pedro.

Pedro turned on his heel and looked at Ken. Then he walked away and leaned his head against a tree.

We stayed like that for what seemed like forever, Pedro against the tree and me and Ken standing around down the street from him. A few people, mostly women, noticed us, but everybody else was too busy going about their own business.

Enero arrived about ten minutes later. He waved to us, and then, seeing Pedro against the tree, went over to him. I watched him put his arm around his nephew, and I watched Pedro pull away from him. I went over to where they were standing.

"There's a stick of dynamite on the motorbike," I said.

"What are you saying?" Pedro's uncle looked at me and then at Pedro.

"Come on, we'll show you," Ken said. He had his nerve back again.

We took Uncle Enero into the shop. I looked around and saw that Pedro had at least turned around to see what we were doing. When we were inside I lifted the fringed flap of leather so that Enero could see the dynamite.

He jumped back at first, one hand in front of my chest and the other over his own heart. Then he looked again. He leaned over and looked from both sides of the dynamite. He went around the bike and looked from the other side. Then he picked up the dynamite, turned it in his hand, and shrugged.

"It's not connected with anything," he said. "There are wires stuck on the side of it, but that's all. I used to work in Italy in a mine. I know about dynamite. This stick has no blasting cap to set it off. Did you take anything off it?"

"No," I said. "The bike conked out on us, and we were trying to get it going again when we found this."

"I'll fix the bike later," Enero said. "Now I'm going to take this to the police!"

"Could you fix the bike now?" Ken asked. "Or at least see what's wrong with it?"

"We got to take the dynamite to the police!" Pedro said. He was standing in the doorway.

"I think he's right," I said. "Blasting cap or no blasting cap, it's still dynamite."

"Maybe," Ken said. "I guess Uncle Enero couldn't figure out what was wrong with the bike anyway."

"Let's get this to the police," Pedro said. Enero looked at Ken, then at me.

I didn't move. I didn't know what my baby brother had in mind, but I knew he was smart, sometimes freaky smart.

Enero looked at us again and then put the stick of dynamite down in a corner in an empty spark plug box. He started looking over the bike quickly, clucking his tongue as he announced that one thing or another wasn't wrong.

"The spark plugs are all right," he said.

He tried to start the bike, listened, and then clapped a big hand to his forehead.

"Pedro, did you take the gas out to sell so you could buy sweets?"

"No!" Pedro said. "Chris and Ken were with me all the time."

"That's right," I said.

Enero looked at the bike again. Then he shook his head. "Look!" he said.

We looked at where he was pointing. The gas line was cut!

Ken and I let Pedro and his uncle go to the police with the dynamite, and we went back to the hotel. I didn't know what wheels were spinning in Ken's head, but I could see that some were.

"You want to tune me in on your brain waves, or are you having a private party?" I asked.

"If the gas line was cut, it meant that whoever put the dynamite on the bike knew it was going to be harmless," Ken said.

"How do you figure that, spaghetti brain?"

"Because if they cut the gas line, they knew we couldn't ride the bike anymore," Ken said. "Then they knew we'd be looking to see what was wrong with the bike and find the dynamite."

"You're saying that someone wants to scare us?" I asked.

"Yes," Ken said. "But since we don't know anything, I wonder why."

When I woke in the morning, Ken's bed was empty and I heard noises in the other room. I wondered what he was doing up, and I threw a shoe at the door. Mom stuck her head in.

"Good morning," she said. "Is that a new primitive custom of greeting in the tribe?"

"When did you get back?"

"Last night." Mom came into the room and leaned against the side of the door. "I've decided to take Sundays off. The families I'm with are barely tolerant of my being with them during the week. They keep their Sundays special, and I have to respect that. Where's Ken?"

"Probably out walking," I said. "There's an ice cream parlor in town, and you know how Ken is about ice cream."

"Your father was like that, too," Mom said. "Sometimes I think it's Ken's genes, and sometimes I think he devours as much ice cream as he does just to try to be like his father."

"He's got this theory that he's the spitting image of Dad, anyway."

"And what's your theory?"

"I can't believe that my father's ears stuck out as much as Ken's," I said.

"You want to go see if we can find some breakfast?"

It was a good idea. I hadn't sat down with Mom since we had reached Spain. I got dressed, and we went to the hotel restaurant. There were lots of families there, some, I'm sure, who weren't staying at the hotel.

"The more I find out about families," Mom said, "the fewer differences I see. What does happen is that the particular area or culture places its own emphasis on things, or—Am I boring you, Chris?"

"Mom, don't turn around right now, but take a look at that guy in the corner, the one wearing the dark suit."

"Is this an intrigue?" Mom asked, picking up a roll and turning it in her fingers. She lowered her head slightly before turning it.

"You see him?"

"Yes."

"We were talking to him the other day, and he asked about you, what kind of work you did, that kind of thing."

"And?"

"He seemed a little peculiar, that's all," I said. "He says he's a historian. He says he's looking for some kind of crown. A Visigoth king owned it at one time. Said if we heard anything about it to let him know."

"If he's very serious about his work," Mom said, "he might certainly appear peculiar. It's not every day that someone devotes himself to events that have happened hundreds of years ago. As far as the Visigoths are concerned, as a matter of fact, it would most likely be well over a thousand years ago."

31

We had breakfast and then went for a short walk in the gardens of the palace. It was full of tourists, and I couldn't find a decent picture, but Mom insisted I take some anyway.

"You know, these pictures won't do an awful lot to build my reputation as a photographer," I said.

"But you'll have your mother's eternal gratitude," Mom said, which meant that she was going to put them in one of the large blue books she called her adventure albums.

By noon it was hot, and we went back to the hotel. Mom made small talk, but I felt she was worried. Ken wandered in about one o'clock and said that he had made a survey of the town and found that they had two souvenir shops for every one person.

"And how many did you buy out?" Mom asked.

Ken emptied his pockets to show that he hadn't bought anything.

I found out why Mom was uncomfortable. The Spanish anthropologist she was working with was taking the whole team across the strait to Tangiers in the morning.

"I just don't like the idea of going to another country and leaving you guys here," she said.

"It's not like you're going to Timbuktu," Ken said. "How long does it take to get to Tangiers? An hour by plane?"

"I'll call you when I get to the university there, which should be about one in the afternoon," Mom said. "Please do me a favor and be here so I can talk to you."

We promised to be in the room when she called and not to fight. We hadn't really had a serious fight in years, so I figured Mom was just trying to get us to take care of each other.

She left early the next morning. It was raining so we played hearts until the phone rang. When it did, Mom talked to Ken for a while and then to me and asked me to see if I could buy a map of the area.

When the rain stopped, we decided to go and find Pedro. We found someone sooner than we expected, but it wasn't Pedro. A very pale but large man was standing outside our door.

"You—you looking for somebody?" I asked.

He smiled slightly, or it could have been just a twitching of his lips—I wasn't sure. I was sure when he turned and walked down the stairs that I didn't like him hanging out outside our door.

Halfway down the hill a small car pulled up near us and the driver asked us if we wanted a lift to town. It was the hotel's car, and we took it. He let us out near the plaza, and Ken said that we should stop in at the telegram place again.

"You still thinking about sending a telegram to Ian?" I asked.

"I did it," Ken said. "I phoned it in from the hotel— that way it didn't go through this office. The lady said it'll be on our bill."

"Mom say you could?" I asked.

"I'll tell her it was your idea," he said.

That ticked me off, because I knew he would. But I also wanted to see if he had received an answer.

We got to the telegraph office, and it was empty. It still smelled of the fire, and I could see that somebody had done a messy job of cleaning up the charred papers. There was a pile of messages on the desk, and Ken looked through them. There was also what looked like a teletype machine, maybe a little fancier, with a continuous roll of paper coming from it. I looked at it and saw that the last message was addressed to Mister Kenneth Arrow.

"Here it is, Ken," I said.

"What's it say?"

> NO CRUZADA CROSS IN ANY REFERENCE SOURCE
> KNOWN TO ANYONE HERE STOP RODERICK'S CROWN
> NOT IN GRANADA

The name on the message was Ian, Ken's friend.

"Here comes the guy who runs the place," Ken said.

I moved away from the teletype machine and pretended to be looking at a Spanish newspaper when the clerk came in.

"You want something?" he asked. He stood in front of the teletype machine as he spoke.

"I just wondered if I've received a telegram," Ken said.

"None in this morning," was the quick reply. "The lines are down."

"Perhaps we'll come back later," I said, before Ken could protest. "In an hour or so."

"That's good," the clerk said. "In an hour."

He was already pushing us out the door, and soon we were back on the sunny streets of Granada.

"But we *saw* the message," Ken said when the clerk had returned to the office. "We saw it!"

"Right, but he doesn't know we saw it," I said. "He's either weird or he's up to something."

Ken gave me a look, and I knew he thought I was pretty weird, too.

We walked around for a bit, then finally headed toward
the telegraph office. This time the clerk was smiling.

"Your telegram did arrive," he said.

Ken took it, read it, and stuck it in his pocket. Outside
the telegraph office he handed it to me, and I read it.

NO CRUZADA CROSS IN ANY REFERENCE SOURCE
KNOWN TO ANYONE HERE STOP RODERICK'S CROWN
A DISTINCT POSSIBILITY STOP SEND DETAILS

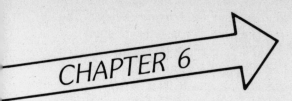

CHAPTER 6

My father disappeared on a trip to Mexico when I was only four. The Mexican government thought that his plane must have gone down in the jungle. Mom said that Ken is a lot like my father. I wondered about that as Ken explained his plan to me and Pedro.

"Bauer has to have something to do with it," Ken said. "He's the only one who knows about the crown. Bauer must have convinced the clerk to change Ian's answer."

"I still think it's risky searching his room," I said.

"That's why one of us will be downstairs to see when he comes back," Ken said. "Whoever's in the lobby will call the room on the house phone, and the other two guys can get out."

"Okay, you watch the lobby," I told Ken. "And whistle twice into the phone if you see Bauer. That way the desk clerk won't know what's going on."

The three of us staked out the front of the hotel until we saw Bauer leave. We waited long enough to see him get into a taxi, and then Ken went to the lobby while Pedro and I went into the hotel through a side door.

I didn't know how we were going to get into Bauer's room. In fact, the only thing I was sure of was that I was nervous. We tried the door. It was locked.

It was an old hotel, and the door didn't look very sturdy. I was thinking about trying to force it when Pedro pointed up. I looked up and saw that there was a transom over the door. It was partially open. I gave Pedro a boost and he wriggled his way through the narrow opening. A moment later he had opened the door for me.

All the rooms in the hotel were large, and Bauer's room was no exception. I figured we had to split the room in half to search it quickly. I had also forgotten to tell Pedro that I wanted everything left as neat as possible. That way Bauer wouldn't know we had ever searched his room.

I was just about to tell Pedro when we heard a flushing sound from the bathroom. We weren't alone!

We got to the door quickly, just in time to hear two whistles from the hallway. Pedro stopped dead in his tracks and looked at me. Then, faster than I could blink, he dove to the floor and under the bed.

There was a closet, the kind you step into, and I jumped into it just as the door opened.

At first I pinned myself against the wall, then I thought that someone might open the closet so I crouched behind some clothing.

There were voices coming from the other room.

"Give me my German passport," a rather high voice, unmistakably that of Erich Bauer, said.

There was a low grunt in reply and footsteps toward the closet. I burrowed deeper into the darkness and pulled a coat in front of myself.

The door to the closet opened, and I could hear some muffled noises above me. There was a loud thumping, too, but it was only my own heart beating about as hard as it ever had. The door to the closet closed, and I listened as hard as I could, but I couldn't make out what they were saying. I imagined the worst—that they knew I was in the closet and were plotting ways of getting rid of my body!

For a while there was silence. Then I heard the sound of a radio being played. I knew I had to do something. If I stayed in the closet they had to find me sooner or later.

I worked my way to the front of the closet and listened. All I heard was the radio. They were playing rock songs in Spanish. I took a breath and eased the closet door open. At first I couldn't see most of the room; then I noticed that I could see the mirror. In the mirror I could just about see the whole room. I wasn't interested in most of it, just the guy on the bed.

It was the same guy I had seen outside our room the day before. I had heard voices, so I knew that someone else had been in the room with him. Had it been Bauer? And how had Bauer gotten past Ken without his seeing him and warning us?

I looked at the bottom of the bed, and I thought I saw Pedro's foot. We were in big trouble.

The guy on the bed got up and walked toward a dresser. He opened it and took out a bottle of something. He sat back on the bed, opened the bottle, and took a big drink.

The phone rang and I stepped backward into the closet. The guy on the bed picked the phone up without speaking. Then he slammed it down! I edged nearer the closet door, wondering if I should make a break for it. Perhaps if I got into a struggle with the guy, Pedro could get out.

I waited for what seemed forever before inching the closet door open and looking at the room through the mirror again. El Creepo was still on the bed, but he looked as if he was dozing. The phone rang again. This time he started for it, then changed his mind and turned over on the bed. I didn't see Bauer anywhere around.

I looked down and saw that Pedro had spotted me looking out of the closet. He pointed up to the top of the bed and shrugged. He wanted to know what the guy on the top of the bed was doing. I took a look. He looked as if he was sleeping. I opened the closet door a little more and made signs of taking a nap.

Pedro came from under the bed. He crawled quickly to the door and opened it. In a moment he was out of the room.

I felt terrible. Pedro had been only a few feet from the door. I had to go clear across the room to get out. Something deep inside me said that I would never see my next birthday. I was hoping that the phone would ring again. It did. I watched El Creepo on the bed. He didn't move.

I waited for another moment before slipping out of the closet and getting down on my hands and knees. I figured if he opened his eyes he would stare straight up at the ceiling. I crawled across the floor slowly, sweat pouring from the sides of my face. When I reached the door, I stood up slowly. I didn't want anyone to see me crawling out of the room. On the other hand, I didn't want to be found out, either.

I was just about to open the door when I saw several passports on the desk beside it. I took a quick look at the sleeping figure on the bed and then took a look at the passports. They all had pictures of Bauer in them, but they all had different names.

I put them down and opened the door.

The hallway was empty, and I got to the stairs as quickly as I could. I went down the stairs three at a time until I got to the landing leading to the lobby. Ken was there. He was white as a ghost. He had his fingers to his lips and he pointed down with his other hand. I stopped next to him and looked over the banister. I saw Captain Rodriguez and two of his policemen. They were putting handcuffs on Pedro!

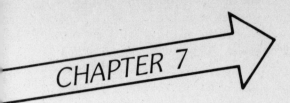

CHAPTER 7

"I was sitting in the lobby, pretending to read a magazine," Ken said. "Then all of a sudden Bauer comes rushing in and heads right for the elevator. I look at the phone, and there's some Spanish lady talking on it, so I ran upstairs, but by the time I got there Bauer was headed toward the room. I whistled from the staircase."

"It's a good thing you did, too. We were just on our way out. You remember that guy we saw outside the room the other day?"

"Yeah?"

"He was in the bathroom when we went into Bauer's room. When we heard your whistle, Pedro got under the bed and I hid in the closet."

"I guess you didn't have a chance to search the room?"

"No, but I did see one thing. Bauer must have half a dozen passports."

"I was really worried about you, Chris." Ken looked as if he wanted to cry. I put my arm around his shoulders and asked him what happened to Pedro.

"I didn't know what to do when I saw Bauer go into the room," Ken said, "so I went back downstairs and waited until the woman got off the phone, then I kept calling. Somebody answered and I whistled, but they just hung up."

"That was El Creepo."

"Then Captain Rodriguez came in. He was talking to the desk clerk, and I thought that maybe I should tell him that you were up there—then I saw Pedro coming down the stairs, and Captain Rodriguez got him and took him away. But I thought he looked surprised to find him here."

"He still took him away," I said.

Pedro was released later that afternoon and went to his Uncle Enero's. When we got to Enero's shop, Pedro told us that he had been formally charged with stealing the Cruzada Cross. He was told that he could not leave Granada without informing Captain Rodriguez. Uncle Enero was in charge of him, and he couldn't leave, either.

"What did the police say to you?" Ken asked.

"They said I might as well confess," Pedro said. "They know I am guilty."

"But you're not guilty!" Ken said. "And I know that."

"But I might confess anyway," Pedro said. "That way my family will not be looked down upon."

Pedro wasn't thinking straight. We tried to get him to have lunch with us, but he wouldn't. He was really upset.

Then Ken said he needed something to steady his nerves, so we headed toward the ice cream shop.

"I don't think he's guilty," Ken said, planning his attack on a dish piled high with ice cream and fruit. "But I'm not sure."

"With all the funny things going on around here," I said, "how can you think Pedro could be guilty?"

"You remember that telegram I sent to Ian?" Ken asked.

"Yes, I do," I said. "I also remember that Ian's answer was changed by the clerk before he gave it to us."

"Ian's really keen on things like that," Ken said. "And his father is a professor at the college in Dover. If the cross had any kind of value, he would have known about it. The only person who would think a cross like that would have value would be someone who thought it was really gold."

"Like Pedro," I said.

"Like Pedro," Ken replied.

"Then how do you explain the guy in Bauer's room?" I asked. "And how do you explain all those passports?"

"I don't," Ken said. "But why would these guys want to steal a worthless cross?"

"Because your friend Ian was wrong," I said. "And Bauer really isn't interested in some Visigoth crown—he's interested in the Cruzada Cross."

Ken has all these friends around his age. Most of them are fourteen, and some of them are as young as twelve. They all consider themselves super kids or something, and I knew that Ken didn't believe that Ian was wrong. I didn't know what to believe.

We got back to the hotel early, and there was a lot of

excitement going on. I spoke to one of the boys who carried bags and asked him what was happening.

"I think the cross must have been returned," he said. "Father Damion said that he had an important announcement to make tonight."

If the cross was returned, it would be great. Then Pedro would be off the hook.

"Unless," Ken said, "it was returned because they found Pedro with it."

The announcement was supposed to be made at the church that evening. Ken and I had dinner at the hotel and waited around, watching Spanish television, until it was time to go to the church. Mom was back from Tangiers and with Profesora Velásquez again. She called and asked how we were doing.

"Okay," I heard Ken saying. "I was just wondering if I should change my shirt before going to church."

Mom said that he probably should, and I knew that she was impressed that he was going to church on a Monday.

The church was full, and everybody seemed fairly happy when we got there. The service was quite lovely, but I didn't see the cross. In fact, the spotlight on the small table where it had sat made its absence even more obvious.

"My children, my friends, my brothers and sisters." Father Damion had spoken to the large audience in Spanish, and everybody had cheered. Then he spoke briefly in English. "I am happy to announce that, although the Cruzada Cross has not been returned, we have been blessed with an anonymous gift with which we can replace the cross with one equally wonderful.

"I cannot express the joy I felt in my heart when I discovered, lying upon the altar this morning, this wondrous gift. The message that came with it was simple. 'Use this for the good of the church.' Some devout person, without ever revealing his name, has given us more than enough pesetas to replace the cross. The remainder of the money we will use to help the poor."

Ken looked at me and I looked at him. Who would give the money? And why in such a strange way?

"Some people are very good," Ken said as we left.

"And very generous," I said. "I heard some people saying that the gift was over a thousand dollars."

"Then we know it wasn't Pedro who gave the gift," Ken said. "Did you see him tonight?"

"No, did you?"

"He might still be down and hasn't heard about this," Ken said. "You want to go tell him?"

I did, and we set out for his uncle's shop.

CHAPTER 8

"*¡Hola!*" Pedro's Uncle Enero was sitting in front of the shop playing dominoes with a friend. "How are you?"

"Fine," I said. "Is Pedro about?"

"No," Enero said. "But he left a message for you in case you came by. He said to tell you that he heard about the gift to the church, and it makes him very sad."

"Sad? Why?" Ken asked.

"He thinks that people will buy a new cross, but they will always think that he has stolen the old one," Enero said. "He went home to the house to see about Violetta. You can talk to him when he returns this evening."

"Violetta?"

"His goat. She knows her way around the village," Enero said. "But Pedro likes to check on her from time to time."

I guessed that Violetta meant the same thing to Pedro that Ken's stuffed frog meant to him. Mom said that Ken would give up the frog sooner or later, and I imagined that Pedro would eventually feel differently about Violetta. But Pedro was right about one thing. The money that was donated for the new cross would take everybody's mind off the old one. I couldn't help thinking that somebody would want just that!

We got back to the hotel and had started through the lobby when I noticed El Creepo sitting in a corner sipping tea. I nudged Ken and started toward the stairs. Ken followed close behind.

"What's up?" he whispered hoarsely.

I was watching El Creepo out of the corner of my eye as Ken and I started up the stairs. He stood up and headed for the elevator.

"Hold it!" I said to Ken. "Remember the guy I told you I saw in Bauer's room?"

"Yes," Ken said.

"That was him sitting across from us. I think he might be following us," I said. "Let's go back downstairs."

We turned and went back down to the lobby. He was nowhere in sight.

"Let's sit for a while," I said. "Unless I'm wrong, El Creepo got into the elevator after we started up the stairs."

"I don't think he's following us," Ken said.

We watched as the elevator indicator stopped on our floor.

"On the other hand"—Ken rubbed his nose with the flat of his palm—"you could have something."

We sat down near a wide column where we could watch the elevator.

"You think he's really following us?" Ken asked.

"Why? You nervous?" I asked.

We watched the elevator. It was coming down again.

"Did I tell you that I would volunteer as your photographic assistant for a small payment?" Ken asked.

The door to the elevator opened. It was empty. Ken relaxed instantly. For a moment I did, too. But seconds later my very wide, very pale friend came running down the stairs. He stopped when he saw us sitting at the table, and he smiled. It was not a nice smile.

"Don't look now," I said. "But the guy I thought was following us is headed this way."

Ken looked immediately and saw the big man lumber toward us.

"Yes, yes, may I join you?" He spoke with a thick accent.

"Sure," Ken said, looking at me.

"It's nice to see young people enjoying themselves," he continued. "I often see the three of you laughing among yourselves."

"The three of us?" Ken said. "I only see me and Chris here."

"Yes, yes. Well, of course, but don't you have another friend? He looks vaguely Spanish. Is he?"

"I don't think I got your name," I said.

His face changed from a barracuda smile to a look that was almost evil. His lips moved several times, as if he was thinking of what he was going to say and his mouth was practicing. Then he smiled again.

"Schumacher," he said. "Otto Schumacher."

"Pleased to meet you," Ken said.

"May I buy a drink?" Schumacher asked.

"We were just about to go up to our room," I said. "Are you staying in the hotel?"

"Yes," he said. "Are the three of you staying in the hotel as well?"

"Yes," Ken answered before I could tell him not to. "Pedro only stays with us once in a while, though."

"And the other times?" Schumacher leaned forward.

"Why don't you ask him when you see him?" I said, getting up.

"Yes, yes. Of course, of course." Schumacher's eyes shifted around. "I suppose I'll see you later? Are you on vacation?"

"No," I said.

I started toward the elevator, hoping Ken would follow. I looked back after I had pressed the button. Schumacher was still talking to Ken. Ken was standing and backing away, and then he came to the elevator.

"What did he say?"

"He said he thinks he must have offended you," Ken said.

"I don't like the looks of that guy," I said.

When we got to our room, we put the chain on the door. It didn't seem very sturdy.

That afternoon it rained. When the rain stopped it got cool, and we had dinner in the hotel restaurant. Then, because we couldn't think of anything better to do, we went looking for Pedro.

He hadn't been at his uncle's shop, but Uncle Enero said that he thought Pedro was still home, and he lent us the motorbike.

"I fixed the gas line," he said. "You shouldn't have anything to worry about."

I looked the bike over carefully, just in case, and then we started out toward Pedro's house. We reached the small house Pedro had told us his grandfather had built years before. The lights were out, and it seemed deserted. Ken and I knocked and then called, but there was no answer.

I pushed the door, and it opened slowly. Ken and I exchanged glances. I found the light switch, and soon the small room we were standing in was filled with an amber light.

"Everything seems to be in place," Ken said. He looked in the other room, and it seemed to be okay, too.

"Let's get back to his uncle's with the bike," I said. "Maybe Pedro went back there."

"And left his house unlocked?"

"It could happen," I answered.

"How about this?" Ken picked up a small sheet of paper from the table. There were red stains on it that could have been blood.

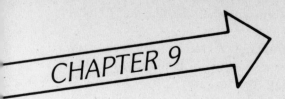

CHAPTER 9

The spots didn't have to be blood. Then again, they didn't have to be red ink, either. Ken looked at the paper, his hands behind his back.

"You afraid of smudging the fingerprints?" I asked.

"Just don't want to get mine on it," Ken said. "Do you know anybody named Leon?"

"Leon? No," I answered. "What does the note say?"

"It's in Spanish," Ken said. "The only thing I recognize is the name Leon."

I looked at the neatly written note and tried to piece it together from the Spanish I had taken in school. I was sure of only two things—*Fuente de Leónes* meant Fountain of Lions, and *peligroso* meant danger.

"We're going to have to get somebody to read this to us," I said. "Somebody who understands Spanish well."

Pedro was nowhere to be found. We looked around the

room and didn't find anything else, except a handkerchief that Ken said was probably Pedro's.

"It smells of benzene or something," he said. "Probably from his uncle's garage."

We took the note off the table and headed back to town. I felt as if everyone we saw was watching us. I could tell that Ken was feeling the same way.

Uncle Enero, as usual, wasn't in his shop. There was a *farmacia*, a drugstore, down the street, and we went there. A very pretty girl, a little shorter than Ken, was behind the counter. We asked her if she spoke English, and she said she did.

"Can you read this note for us?" I asked.

She looked at it, then shrugged.

"It doesn't make much sense. I think a teacher wrote it," she said. "It says, 'Bring it to the Fountain of Lions at midnight or you will be in much trouble.' "

"Why do you think a teacher wrote it?" Ken asked.

"It's like school Spanish," the girl said. "It's not written the way most Spanish people write."

We bought some toothpaste and left.

"What do you think the 'it' meant?" Ken asked. "The cross?"

"Probably," I said. "That would make sense. What doesn't make sense is bringing it to the Fountain of Lions at midnight."

"That sounds like a code word or something," Ken said.

"No, the Fountain of Lions is on the Alhambra grounds. But the palace is closed up in the evenings. So even if Pedro did have the cross he couldn't bring it there at midnight."

"Maybe whoever wrote the note doesn't really want him to bring it there," Ken said. "I mean it is a funny place to bring something. Why doesn't he just say leave it on the table in Pedro's house?"

"How do I know?" We were waiting for the bus to go back to the hotel.

"Of course," Ken said, turning his head sideways the way he did when he thought he had a good idea, "if I wanted something from Pedro I might want him to bring it to me instead of going to his place where someone might see me."

"But whoever wrote the note has already gone to Pedro's place," I said. "And why would they care how they got the cross *back* as long as they got it *back*? Sounds like a setup to me."

The bus lumbered around the corner, and we began waving frantically for it to stop. Sometimes the bus would stop on schedule at all the stops, and sometimes the driver would just look at us as he passed us. A waiter at the hotel said that if we really wanted a bus in Granada, we should chase it, and we started after it as it went by us. The driver let us run for a while before stopping.

"You're out of breath," Ken said.

"I am not," I panted.

"Suppose they don't want it back?" Ken said. "Suppose they don't want to give the cross back to the church?"

"Then they wouldn't have Pedro bringing it to them in the middle of the night so everyone could see it," I said.

"I guess you're right," Ken said. "But since the hotel is right across from the palace, we can see if Pedro brings—"

Ken stopped talking and looked at me. We both hit on

it at the same time. If Pedro did bring anything to the palace, anyone could spot him from the hotels that faced the palace ground! "Why would anyone think that he would bring the cross after all this time?" Ken asked. "But what else would anyone want from Pedro?"

That part made no sense at all. The whole thing was like a giant crossword puzzle without the black squares or numbers. There seemed to be a lot of things going on, but we didn't know where to put them. One thing we did decide was to stay up and watch the entrance of the palace. It seemed the obvious thing to do. It also seemed fairly simple. It turned out not to be.

"Ah, there you are!" Mr. Bauer was leaning on the hotel desk when we entered the lobby. "I've been looking all over for you two."

"What for?" I asked.

"I'm quite tired of dining alone," Bauer said. "And I thought you two would make the most perfect dinner companions."

"I'm afraid we're really kind of tired," I said.

"Then a good dinner will refresh you!" Bauer replied quickly.

In a moment we were in the elevator, and Bauer had pushed the button for the dining room floor.

"Why don't you two go ahead?" Ken said. "I'll wash up a bit and join you in the dining room."

"Splendid!" Bauer was all smiles and twinkles.

Ken got off on our floor and I went up to the dining room with Bauer.

We settled at a table away from the window, and Bauer told the waiter who came over that we were expecting one more and that we would wait before ordering.

"And how do you like your holiday in Spain?" he asked.

"Fine," I said. "And how's your work coming?"

"My work?" He smiled. "It's coming quite well. I forgot that your mother was an anthropologist. I should have expected you to inquire about my work."

Bauer made small talk while we waited for Ken. He was trying hard to seem friendly. He asked a few questions about Mom's work, too, but I didn't think he was interested in my answers. Ken showed up pretty quickly, and Bauer signaled for the waiter to bring menus. He also said that he would pay for our dinner.

"I have a son and a daughter," Bauer said. "They're just a bit older than you two, I imagine."

"Where are they now?" Ken asked.

"They're in Switzerland." Bauer picked up the large menu. "Did I tell you I was Swiss?"

"No," Ken said.

Ken picked up his menu and held it in front of him. He glanced at Bauer and then pointed down at the table. I lifted my eyebrows as slightly as I could to let him know that I didn't know what he meant.

Then he reached into his pocket and pulled out the keys.

"I think I'm going to choose the special of the day," Bauer said.

"What is it?" I asked. "My Spanish isn't that good."

As soon as Bauer picked up the menu again to read me what the special was, Ken started pointing down again. He had taken the keys out so I figured that he meant our room. Then he made a letter *P* on the table. Pedro was in our room!

I ordered the special, which was fish, and Ken made Mr. Bauer go through the menu until he found something that sounded vaguely like a hamburger, and he ordered that. I envied him.

"So how do you amuse yourself when your mother is in the field?" Mr. Bauer asked after the food had been served.

"Sightseeing, mostly," Ken said. "And Chris takes lots of pictures. He thinks he's going to sell some of them when we get home."

"Hmm. That could be, but you couldn't possibly spend all your time sightseeing and taking pictures," Bauer said.

"And just walking around," I said. "Do you have other suggestions?"

"I just thought two bright young men like yourselves would be involved in some kind of adventure," Bauer chuckled. "Don't tell me you haven't found *anything* to amuse yourselves."

"We were thinking about looking for King Roderick's crown," Ken said.

"Is that so?" Bauer stopped eating and looked first at Ken and then at me as if he was trying to figure out if we were telling the truth.

I wondered why Pedro was in our room. I was thinking about pretending to have forgotten something and telling Bauer that I was going down to the room to look for it. Then I saw Ken's eyes widen. He gave me a look and then looked down at his plate.

"Excuse me," Bauer said. "I have to visit the rest room. Continue eating, I'll only be a minute or two,"

As soon as he left I asked Ken what was up.

"That guy that followed us up the stairs the other night just came into the dining room," Ken said. "He touched his nose and then headed toward the rest room."

"And then Bauer went in there to meet him!" I said. "Do you think he knows that Pedro is here?"

"I don't think so," Ken said. "Pedro says that he's been keeping out of sight since he found the note."

"Does he know what it means?"

"He says he doesn't," Ken said. "But he found the note in the little pen in the back of his house where he kept Violetta, his goat. And now the goat's missing!"

"Watch it," I said, under my breath. "Here's our friend."

"Well, it doesn't even look as if you boys even touched your food," Bauer said, returning to the table. "Don't you like Spanish cuisine?"

CHAPTER 10

Ken and I tried our best to be casual with Bauer, but it wasn't easy. He never mentioned Pedro, but we could tell he was wondering how much we knew. I wanted to tell Ken not to talk too much, but I didn't have to—he was eating. When dinner was finally over, we excused ourselves and went down to our room. Pedro looked terrible. His hands were shaking, and I could see that he had been crying.

"Are you okay?" I asked.

"They'll probably eat her." Pedro shook his head sadly.

"Eat who?"

"They took Violetta, my goat," Pedro said. "She was tied in the back, and now she's gone. Did you see the blood?"

"Violetta's?" I asked.

Pedro nodded.

"But you don't know that they actually killed her, do you?"

Pedro shook his head.

"Do you have a white handkerchief that smells of benzene or something?" Ken asked.

"No, he doesn't," I answered for Pedro. "That wasn't benzene on the handkerchief—that was something they used to knock the goat out when they kidnapped her."

"You don't think Violetta is dead?" Pedro asked.

"I don't know," I said. "But the important thing is that maybe whoever went there didn't go for the goat. Maybe they went for you!"

"I would have strangled him with my bare hands!" Pedro said.

"What really bugs me," Ken said, "is why someone still thinks that Pedro has the cross."

"And what really bugs me," I said, "is *who* thinks that he has it. It doesn't make sense. Whoever took the goat must have searched your house and knows it's not there."

"His Uncle Enero is always out so they could easily have searched the shop, too," Ken said.

"The note said to bring the cross to the Fountain of the Lions," I said. "Think hard. Does that mean anything special to you?"

"I can't bring the cross to the Fountain of the Lions if I don't have it," Pedro said. "And you can't climb over the gate anyway because there are guards there."

"Chris doesn't think they want you to bring it to the fountain," Ken said. "He thinks somebody doesn't know who has the cross and maybe left notes all over town."

"Then they follow whoever brings it and get him," I said.

"That sounds like Captain Rodriguez," Ken said.

"We had dinner with Bauer tonight." I took my shoes off and sat cross-legged on the bed. "He looked about as suspicious as anybody. El Creepo could have been watching the gates while Bauer had dinner with us.

"I wish we had something to make them show their hand," I said. "If we knew who we were dealing with at least, it would be good."

"Maybe I could put that old picture right in front of the gates," Pedro said. "Then—"

"What picture?" Ken and I interrupted at the same time.

"You remember I said that a woman came in and she looked like a saint?"

"I remember," I said. "Go on."

"Well, when she was gone so quickly I thought maybe I was imagining the whole thing. I saw her touch the picture in back of the altar just as I called to her. When she disappeared, I thought I would look at the picture to see if maybe it would glow or something. It didn't glow or anything, but I wanted to look at it again."

"Why would it glow?" Ken asked.

"If she was a saint, it would glow," Pedro said.

"Then what did you do?" I asked.

"I was going to take it back later, but when I got back to the church and they accused me of stealing the cross, I took the picture to my uncle's shop and put it under the seat in his pickup truck."

"Is it still there?" Ken asked.

"I think it is," Pedro said.

"Well, either they found it and think you have the cross because you had the picture," I said, "or it's the picture they're looking for. Why didn't you tell us about this picture before?"

"Not important," Pedro said. "It's an old picture and very dirty."

"We'll find out if the picture is still there tomorrow," I said. "Meanwhile, let's make sure the door is locked well tonight."

The telephone ringing woke us early in the morning. I got there first and found that it was just Mom checking in with us.

"We're doing fine," I said. "We still have a problem with someone thinking that Pedro might have stolen the Cruzada Cross, though."

"Until it's found people will still think whatever they please," Mom said. "And even though he's your friend, you have to be careful not to offend people. I'm sure the cross meant a great deal to many people."

"You don't often see a picture behind a cross, do you?" I asked Mom.

"Not in modern churches," Mom said. "But centuries ago, when the altar was carved in stone or built into the walls of the church, they would often have carved panels or paintings on the altar. Many were outstanding works of art."

Suddenly things began to make more sense.

"Valuable?" I asked.

"Priceless," Mom said. "Would you like me to get you a book on religious art? I'm sure you'd enjoy it."

"I don't think so," I said. "Maybe later."

"Oh." It was one of Mom's disappointed "oh's." So I said that maybe I wouldn't mind a book on religious art if it wasn't too long.

Mom talked to Ken awhile and then said hello to Pedro.

"Mom said she was getting us some books on religious art," Ken said as we got ready to leave. "That *your* idea?"

We went down to the lobby and got a cab to Uncle Enero's shop. The picture was right where Pedro had said he had put it. It didn't look like much—old, maybe, but not too exciting. His uncle was surprised that it was there. I guessed that it was meant to be a picture of a saint or something.

"A saint?" Uncle Enero held the picture at arm's length and looked at it. "Maybe that's why the truck has been running so good."

"Maybe we should take it to the police," Ken said.

"Then Pedro gets into trouble for taking the picture," I said. "Unless you want to explain to Captain Rodriguez that he took it by mistake."

"No, *gracias*!" Pedro held the picture up to the light and shook his head.

"I don't think it'll help clear Pedro's name to take the picture to Captain Rodriguez right now." Ken was rubbing his nose with the palm of his hand, the way he does when he gets an idea. "But it might, if we plan it carefully, be a good idea to take ourselves to the police. Especially if Uncle Enero is a good driver."

"Me?" Uncle Enero put his stubby finger against his chest. "I am the best!"

It was a wild scheme at first, but I thought it just might work. The four of us sat down and went over the idea enough times to convince ourselves that it would be okay. Uncle Enero gave Ken a funny look, but he agreed that he would try my brother's idea.

Pedro showed up in the lobby of the Washington Irving right on time. He brought a large bag with him, large enough to hold the picture. He sat with me and Ken in the lobby for fifteen minutes before Bauer showed up. Bauer took one look at us and came over quickly. As soon as he headed in our direction, Ken went out the front door of the hotel as planned.

"And how are my young adventurers this evening?" Bauer asked, looking directly into my eyes. He was ignoring Pedro sitting next to me.

"Well . . . er . . . just fine," I said.

Pedro put both of his arms around the package he was carrying, but Bauer didn't seem to notice.

"I must go up for my pills," Bauer said. "I'm not all that used to taking medication, but I must. I have an allergy to something in the air around here. I guess you fellows will be retiring soon?"

"I don't think so," I said as Ken came over to us.

"I have the directions," Ken announced loudly.

Pedro had arrived at the hotel on his uncle's motorbike, and after asking everybody in the lobby, including the desk clerk, if our directions were right, we all piled on the bike. I told Ken to get in the side car first so he could turn and see what Bauer was doing; Bauer was talking to the desk clerk. The plan was working. We headed slowly toward the police station.

We had to wait nearly thirty minutes before Captain Rodriguez showed up. Then, after we had repeated the story we had rehearsed that afternoon five times, it was another forty minutes before Captain Rodriguez's men brought in Señor Abreu, the hotel desk clerk.

"You are a liar! And a thief! And if you have a father, then the pig should disown you!" The desk clerk alternated between English and Spanish so that not only would Pedro know he was being insulted but his two English-speaking friends would know that they were being insulted as well.

"The boys say they saw you with the cross," Captain Rodriguez said.

"I swear I have never seen the cross except at Mass! He is an idiot and he is an idiot and he is an idiot!" The furious desk clerk pointed toward each of us in turn.

Finally, after another half hour during which Ken started shouting back at the clerk, Captain Rodriguez told us all to go home.

"Aren't you going to arrest him?" Ken asked. He had this real innocent look on his face.

"*Señor*"—Captain Rodriguez put his hand on Ken's shoulder—"I don't think you should be with your friend Pedro too much. He sees saints, and now you all see a perfectly honest man doing bad things. Maybe the water in Granada does not agree with you. I suggest you all go home."

The nights in Granada were usually fairly cool, but it

was warm when we left the police station. The police offered Señor Abreu a lift back to the hotel, but he refused. He kept giving Pedro, Ken, and me evil looks and spitting on the ground.

Pedro, still clutching the package he had brought with him to the police station, got on the motorbike and drove off. Ken and I started as if we were headed toward the bus stop, then ducked into a doorway and watched as the lights of a dark car flicked on and started slowly after Pedro.

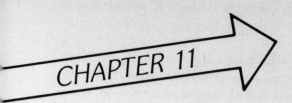

CHAPTER 11

Ken took off his glasses, which was the signal that we had arranged, and we waited, but nothing happened. I looked around the little square to see if I could see Pedro's uncle. Nothing. The plan was to set a trap by showing everybody a package that could have been the painting, but not the cross. Only someone who knew about the painting would be interested. We had made sure that the desk clerk, Bauer, and Captain Rodriguez had all seen the package. Pedro's uncle was to have a car parked out of sight near the square, and if we saw anyone follow Pedro, we would signal and Uncle Enero would bring the car up. Then we would all follow whoever it was who was following Pedro. It had sounded like a foolproof plan.

"You think we have a problem?" Ken asked.

"Looks like it," I said.

Just then there was a tremendous racket as an old bus

careened into the middle of the square. It lurched to an unsteady stop, and I could see who was driving. It was Uncle Enero.

"I am late!" he said.

"What is *that*?" Ken looked at the old bus. There were crates tied to the top of it, and what seemed like the clucking of chickens came from the interior.

"I could not get the car, my friends," Uncle Enero said. "Also, the pickup truck would not start. But the bus is very good and very fast."

I had my doubts, but we got on the bus anyway.

Pedro's uncle knew the roads, which was good. I hoped he knew the bus as well. There were no lights in the bus. Only one of its headlights worked, and the clanking from under the hood sounded as if the engine was ready to abandon the green-and-orange wreck.

Pedro was headed toward the Bridge of Sighs, a small bridge just south of Granada. The legend was that when the Moors were defeated and had to leave Granada, they turned at the bridge to take one last look at their lost kingdom, and their sighs were heard by everyone around.

The streets were nearly empty, but we didn't see any sign of Pedro.

"Maybe nobody followed him," Uncle Enero said.

"We saw a car leave a moment after he did," Ken said.

There was the chicken noise again. This time it sounded as if it was in the back of the bus.

"Where did you get this bus?" I asked.

"I borrowed it from a friend," Enero said. We were stopped for a traffic light. Enero opened the window, stuck his head out, and spoke in Spanish to the driver of the car next to us.

"He said he didn't see anyone come this way on a motorbike," Enero said when he had pulled his head back into the bus.

"I'm sure Pedro wouldn't change the route," Ken said.

"Enero, are there chickens in the back of the bus?" I'm not sure why I asked. There was a chicken walking down the aisle toward us. It walked near where Ken was sitting, clucked twice, and headed for the back of the bus again.

We hit the highway and passed a few cars. I looked to see if I could find the car that had followed Pedro. I realized that I hadn't seen it well enough. Neither had Ken.

"I know it looked mysterious, though," Ken said. "If that's any help."

"It's not," I said.

"Sometimes," Enero said, nodding his head as if he was sharing a great truth with us, "my pickup truck is mysterious. And sometimes it just doesn't want to do anything. But you know, I believe it was doing much better when it had the picture of the saint in it."

We were traveling at nearly eight-five kilometers an hour. The lights we passed flashed across Ken's face. He looked at me and smiled. I tried to smile too, but then I thought of Pedro.

"There! Look up ahead!" Enero said after we had been on the road for nearly fifteen minutes.

At first I didn't see anything. Then, about a kilometer ahead, I saw the motorbike. Ken had gone back to look at the chickens, and I called to him.

"I don't see anyone right behind him," Ken said, as the

motorbike disappeared around a bend in the road. "Maybe no one was following him after all."

"Well, after driving around for an hour or so he's going to be headed back to his house," I said. "If no one followed him, they still might take the bait and go to the house."

"Either way," Enero said, "we keep our eyes on him."

We drove in silence for a while. Enero got fairly close to Pedro, close enough for us to see that he had put the package in the side car. In the car behind Pedro there was a woman, and in the car behind that two men. It was the car with the two men that I figured would be the one if any of the cars was following him.

"There's a car in the other lane with a guy in it," Ken said. "I can't make out what he looks like, though."

It was a small orange *seat*. It pulled up next to Pedro, then fell back, then pulled up next to him again.

"What do you think he's doing?" I asked Enero.

"Maybe trying to look for a way to force him over," Enero said. "I think I'll get a little closer."

Enero pulled into the left lane and edged closer to the *seat*. Ken got on one side of the bus, and I got near the front window to see if we could see who was driving it.

"I'm sure it's a man," Ken said. "He looks kind of young."

From the way he was sitting in the seat, the man looked small, too.

"I can't tell," I said. "It's hard to see inside the car."

Enero edged a little closer. I wasn't sure that was such a good idea. We didn't want to scare away whoever it was before they made some kind of move.

Then the *seat* started to pull away quickly. I looked at

74

the dial on the speedometer. We were on ninety. The *seat* pulled away from us easily.

"I guess he wasn't following Pedro," Enero said.

"Or he caught on to us," Ken said.

"I don't think he knows we're following him," Enero said. "Would you think you were being followed by a bus?"

"It was good the fellow lent it to you," I said.

"When I give it back to him I will tell him that," Enero said. "Right now he doesn't know how good he is being!"

Enero laughed. Ken gave me a look and shook his head.

Just then there was a loud screeching noise up ahead. The car ahead of Pedro had slammed on its brakes just before a small cutoff. We saw Pedro veer off to his right, moving off the road onto the cutoff to avoid the swerving car.

We were passing in the left lane, and we saw the car go off the road and onto the service road behind Pedro.

"Some fool missed the cutoff and almost killed Pedro!" Enero shouted and honked the bus's horn in anger.

I rushed to the back of the bus and pushed a chicken away from the window ledge. The car had stopped on the turnoff and two men were taking Pedro off his bike!

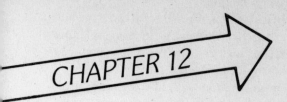

CHAPTER 12

"They've got Pedro!" I shouted. "They were in front of him!"

"Iiee!" Enero let out a cry and looked around for some place to stop the bus. There wasn't any.

"What are we going to do?" Ken's knuckles were white as he gripped the sides of the seat.

"We go back for him!" Enero moved the bus toward the right lane.

"Pedro doesn't have the picture with him," I said. "They'll have to go to the pickup truck to get it."

"Or to his house if he doesn't tell them where it is," Ken said. "Do you think he'll tell?"

"If they threaten to hurt him he will," I said.

"If they hurt Pedro I will tear their tongues from their throats!" Enero said. He jerked the wheel of the bus, sending it screeching into the right lane. Cars honked furiously around us as Enero cut them off.

There was another turnoff a kilometer up the road, and Enero took it with the wheels squealing in protest. I hung on to the seat as crates, chickens, and vegetables bounced around in the dark interior of the old bus.

It took us a few minutes more to get back to the cutoff where they had ambushed Pedro. We had to run across the highway, dodging cars as we did.

The engine of the motorbike was still on when we got there. The cardboard that Pedro had put in the package he was carrying was on the ground next to the tire prints of the car.

"Curse them!" Enero said. "And curse my stupidity!"

"Look, we're sorry," Ken said.

"No, they are the ones who will be sorry," Enero said. The veins bulged in his neck. "I will go back to my shop. Heaven help them if they are there!"

"Let's go," Ken said.

"No." I grabbed Ken's arm. "We'll go to the house. If everything's okay there, we can call the police and tell them to go to Enero's shop!"

Enero went across the road, zigzagging between cars, until he reached the bus. There was a chicken on the hood and he grabbed it and threw it into the bus before jumping in himself. In a moment he was back on the highway.

Ken and I got on the motorbike.

"Chris, you scared?" Ken asked.

"No," I lied.

"Then you're stupid!" he said.

I patted him on the shoulder and pushed the bike into gear.

I didn't know what we were going to do when we reached Pedro's house. I was just hoping that it would be empty and all we would have to do was to call the police. I was thinking of some way of getting Ken out of danger, too. I figured I could handle myself, and I didn't want him getting hurt.

It took us what seemed forever to get to the road to Pedro's house. He lived on a steepish hill, and I suggested that we leave the bike at the bottom of the hill and walk up so that they wouldn't hear us coming.

"No way," Ken said. "We drive up, and if we see their car we don't stop."

That sounded like a better idea, and I took the motorbike up the cobblestoned hill. My heart was beating faster and faster even though I kept telling myself that Pedro had probably told them where the picture was and that by now they probably had it and were gone on their way.

We reached the top of the hill and passed two houses before we reached Pedro's. All the houses on the street were attached, and Pedro's was in the middle of them. There was a cart in front of one of the other houses; otherwise the street was empty.

"You want to look inside?" Ken said.

"Suppose they come when we're in there?" I said.

"We leave the bike outside," Ken said. "When they see that, they'll know it's Pedro's, but they won't know if we've contacted the police, so they'll have to go away."

The kid was a genius.

We parked the bike right in front of Pedro's house so that anyone coming could surely see it. We checked Pedro's door. It was locked.

"The window's open," Ken said.

I gave him a boost and followed as quickly as I could. The place was dark. For a moment. Then the lights went on.

"Well, my friends, I'm glad you have joined us!"

Erich Bauer was seated with his feet on the table. El Creepo, the guy I had seen in his room, stood against the wall. He had one hand on the light switch. The other held a small gun pointed in my direction.

There was a muffled noise from the floor. I looked and saw Pedro, his hands tied, under the table.

"What is being decided now"—Bauer spoke slowly— "is whether you will hand over the painting, or whether we will be forced to kill all of you. Do you have any suggestions?"

"Maybe we should kill one of them," El Creepo said. "Yes, yes, that would get them talking!"

They could have been bluffing, but I wasn't sure. I didn't know what they would do once they got the painting, either.

"I think the painting you want is in his uncle's shop." Ken spoke in a squeaky voice. "In the pickup truck."

Bauer and El Creepo exchanged glances.

"I think you're lying!" Bauer screamed and pounded his fist on the table. "We searched the shop and it's not there! Do you take me for a fool!?"

He swung his feet quickly off the table and stood up. Out of the corner of my eye I saw Ken move. I had just turned my head in his direction when there was what seemed like an explosion above me. I looked up just as something hit me from behind and knocked me to the floor. Two shots rang through the small room as the lights went out. A thousand noises went through my head, and swirling pinpoints of light danced around me.

There were footsteps and heavy breathing in the darkness. I felt a pain in the back of my neck as I shut my eyes.

I forced my eyes open, but I couldn't see in the darkness. From far away I heard a scuffling noise. Then I felt something wet and sticky against my forehead. I knew I was almost unconscious, and it was harder and harder to fight it.

Then the beam of a flashlight danced around the room.

"Where's the other one?" It was El Creepo's voice.

"I don't see him!" I recognized Bauer's voice. "Let's get out of here!"

More footsteps. The sound of a door opening. I realized I was lying on the floor. My head was aching. I was still alive, but I didn't know for how long. Then there was quiet.

I was still on the hard floor, trying to collect my thoughts, to figure out what had happened. I realized I had closed my eyes again. I could hear someone breathing next to me. I didn't want to open my eyes, but I forced myself to. I could see the dim outline of Pedro.

Neither of us moved for a long while.

"Ken?" I called to my brother. "Are you all right?"

There was no answer.

I moved my arm from under my body and pushed myself up. I could make out shadows in the darkness, and some shapes, but that was all. I tried shaking my head to get rid of the cobwebs. Big mistake. I touched my head. It was hurt.

"Ken?" I called again.

I got on my hands and knees and crawled to where Ken had been what seemed only seconds before. I couldn't find him. I finally made it to my feet.

"Pedro?"

Pedro made a noise from under the table. I felt my way to him and worked the gag off his mouth. He took several deep breaths and sniffed.

"There's a knife in the closet in the corner," he said.

"I can't find it in the dark," I answered.

"Then help me up."

His hands were tied behind his back, but his legs weren't tied. I helped him to his feet and then heard him move around.

"Here!" he called to me.

I felt sick, but I went to him. I thought I was going to throw up any moment. I didn't say anything. I was listening for the sound of Ken's breathing.

I felt around until I found a closet. I reached inside until I found the knife, and then, carefully, I cut Pedro's ropes. As soon as I did, I heard him fumbling in the dark. Then he struck a match, and I saw that he had found an oil lamp. He lit it and held it up. I looked around the room. Ken wasn't there.

Pedro put his hand on my face and looked at me closely.

"How come you have an egg on your head?" he asked.

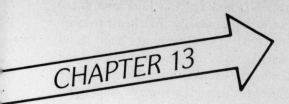

CHAPTER 13

"We have to get to a telephone and get the police!" I just about shouted at Pedro.

"I don't have a telephone," said Pedro, "but there is one down the street."

We rushed outside and looked around. The motorbike was still in front of the house. I took deep breaths of the cool air, trying to calm down, but it wasn't much use.

"You all right?" Pedro asked.

"Yes, but I've got to stay here and look around for Ken," I said. "You go on."

"The telephone is right down the street. We can call the police from there," Pedro said. "Chris, come with me . . . it's best."

"Let's go."

We got to the corner as quickly as we could. Then both of us stopped cold. There was a crowd at the bottom of the hill; people were pointing to something and shouting. A car with flashing lights was parked to one side. I half ran, half stumbled down the hill. By the time I reached the edge of the crowd I was exhausted, and I knew that I must look like a wild man. Pedro was shouting behind me as we fought our way through the crowd. Then I stopped. There in the middle of the crowd, his hands waving furiously as he talked, was Ken. Captain Rodriguez stood next to him, leaning against a van. I recognized the guy being escorted into the back of the van by two policemen. It was El Creepo! I went up to Ken and grabbed him. A policeman tried to separate us, but Captain Rodriguez stopped him. A second later I felt an arm around my shoulders, and Ken and I included Pedro in our embrace.

"It was Schumacher who actually took the cross," Ken was spouting off to Mom. "He actually dressed as a woman so no one would suspect him after he got the painting. But he had to move the cross to get to the painting. He had actually moved the picture from its place when Pedro saw him."

"Schumacher's the one I call El Creepo," I said, from beneath an ice pack.

"But when Pedro called to him he panicked and left, taking the cross with him. He dropped it in a ditch near where he had parked his car. The police went there and found it yesterday."

"But the painting was gone, too," Mom said. "Why didn't anybody report that missing?"

"Because the important thing to everybody was the cross," I said. "No one knew how valuable the painting was. Nobody except Bauer, that is. Bauer was just passing through when he saw it. He recognized that it was valuable, and a few questions here and there showed him that no one else knew that it was. And—"

"So," Ken interrupted, "when they saw that the painting was gone, and that Pedro had been accused of stealing the Cruzada Cross they decided that he must have had the painting."

"Pedro didn't realize that the painting was valuable or he would have taken it back," I said. "He was hoping that when they found the cross he would take the picture back and everything would be fine."

"Captain Rodriguez said that Bauer really was Swiss, but he was known as an art thief all over Europe," Ken said. "Schumacher worked with him."

"Now tell me about thinking that you were shot, Chris," Mom said.

"I was standing there trembling in my boots," I said, "when all of a sudden I heard what sounded like a shot. Then the lights went out, I was going down to the floor, and I felt this terrific pain in my head."

"Mom, pass the toast," Ken said, stuffing another bit of sausage into the endless cavern of his mouth. "And I will explain what happened."

"Let's save some for your brother," Mom said. She pushed the toast away. Ken had already had four pieces. "He hasn't eaten a thing."

"I'm not really hungry," I said, trying to reposition the ice pack on my head.

Mom put the toast back within Ken's reach.

"I tried to figure out what Bauer and El Creepo's next

move would be," Ken said. "We knew who they were, and by that time we knew what they were after. So I guessed that they had to shoot us. It was only logical."

"Not necessarily," Mom said. "Bauer and his friend were already wanted by the police for stealing art works. That's what they do. So being wanted for stealing one more piece wouldn't have bothered them very much."

"Well, it seemed logical," Ken said. "So I had these eggs in my pocket and I took them out and threw them at the light bulb. As soon as I hit it, I knocked Chris down by jumping against the back of his legs. That's when he banged his head on the table. Pedro was already on the floor. Then I crawled into the next room and went through the window before anyone knew what was happening. I was going to go get help as fast as I could. By the time I got down the hill I saw the police coming up the hill."

"When Enero didn't find Pedro at his shop, he called Captain Rodriguez and told him what had happened," I said. "Captain Rodriguez brought his men to Pedro's house and they met Ken at the bottom of the hill. They had left their car down the hill so they wouldn't be spotted. I *told* Ken that was a good idea."

"So you think like a thief," Ken said. "Big deal."

"When Bauer and El Creepo found out that Ken was gone, they got out of there fast and started hot—footing it down the hill, too," I said. "By the time they realized they had made a mistake it was too late."

"Well, I'm certainly glad you didn't miss the light bulb," Mom said. "But what were you doing with the eggs in your pocket?"

"You remember the chickens we told you about?" Ken

brushed the last of the toast crumbs from his mouth. "The ones on the bus?"

"Go on."

"I took the eggs from the basket and I wanted to see what the chicken would do if I put them in my pocket," Ken said sheepishly. "But then everything got crazy and I didn't think about them again until we were in Pedro's house."

"You're still a kid," I said. "Playing with chickens makes you an absolute kid!"

"Yes, but at least I wasn't as embarrassed as you were," Ken said.

"Embarrassed? I wasn't embarrassed," I said.

"Oh? It looked to me as if you had egg on your face," Ken said. "Get it? Egg on your face?"

Mom and I went into the next room and closed the door quietly.

ABOUT THE AUTHOR

Walter Dean Myers has written many novels for young adults including two ALA Notable Books, *Fast Sam, Cool Clyde, and Stuff* and *It Ain't All for Nothin'*, and two ALA Best Books for Young Adults, *The Young Landlords* and *The Legend of Tarik*. Mr. Myers lives in New Jersey.